The Golden Fish

An Old Story from China
Retold by Roslyn Joyce
Illustrated by Marie Low

Lin lives in Beijing, which is the capital city of China. She likes listening to music and reading. Lin's favorite story is *The Golden Fish*. Like Yeh Hsien (*yih SHEN*) in this story, Lin and her friends enjoy going to the Lantern Festival.

In this story from China, we learn that *kindness* deserves a rich reward and that it does not pay to be greedy.

kindness helping others

Long ago in China, there lived a kind and beautiful girl. Her name was Yeh Hsien. Yeh Hsien had a stepmother who made her work all day long.

One day, as Yeh Hsien was getting water from the well, she saw a beautiful, golden fish.

"Please don't hurt me," said the little fish.

Yeh Hsien loved all animals, so she took care of the little fish. She fed it until it was big enough to swim in the pond.

One day, the stepmother saw Yeh Hsien playing with the beautiful, golden fish.

"Yeh Hsien is too happy," she said.

The stepmother put on Yeh Hsien's colorful coat and got a big, sharp knife and went to the pond. Then she called for the golden fish.

The fish jumped up to play. It saw the big, sharp knife, and it was frightened. In a flash, the fish swam away.

frightened afraid of something

Later, Yeh Hsien went to the pond. She called to the fish, but it did not jump up to play. Yeh Hsien was sad and worried. She began to cry, and her tears fell like crystals into the water.

Suddenly, an old man appeared.

"The golden fish will not return," he said, "but do not cry. It is safe. It sends you this magic fish bone."

Soon it was spring and time for the Lantern Festival. Yeh Hsien's stepmother would not let her go. She told Yeh Hsien to stay home and work.

Yeh Hsien was very sad. So she held her magic fish bone and wished for fine clothes. Suddenly, she was wearing a beautiful, silk gown and a pair of satin slippers.

Yeh Hsien decided to go to the festival. When she got there, she saw her stepmother. Frightened, she ran through the crowds, and a slipper fell off!

The lost slipper was brought to the royal palace. When the king saw the slipper, he said, "The person who fits this beautiful slipper shall be my queen."

The slipper was taken all over the land. At Yeh Hsien's house, the stepmother tried to force her big foot into the dainty slipper.

"Let me try," cried Yeh Hsien. The satin slipper fit her perfectly!

dainty fine, delicate, and beautifully made

13

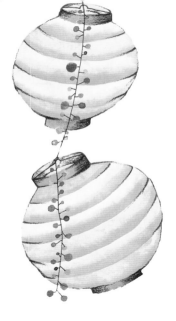

Yeh Hsien put on her silk gown and the matching slipper. She went to the palace and married the happy king.

One day, Yeh Hsien told her husband about the magic fish bone. He was very excited. He wished and wished until the palace was full of beautiful things. Suddenly, the magic stopped.

"You have worn out the magic!" said Yeh Hsien.

The king apologized. He buried the fish bone in the sand, and it was never seen again.

apologize to say you are sorry

15

Discussion Starters

1 Both Yeh Hsien and the king used the magic fish bone to make wishes. Why do you think it stopped working?

2 Does this story remind you of another tale? How is it the same? How is it different?

How did Yeh Hsien show kindness toward the golden fish?